Elfabit

written and illustrated by
STEVE PILCHER

Hayes
Publishing
Ltd.

A is for acorn which makes a small boat.

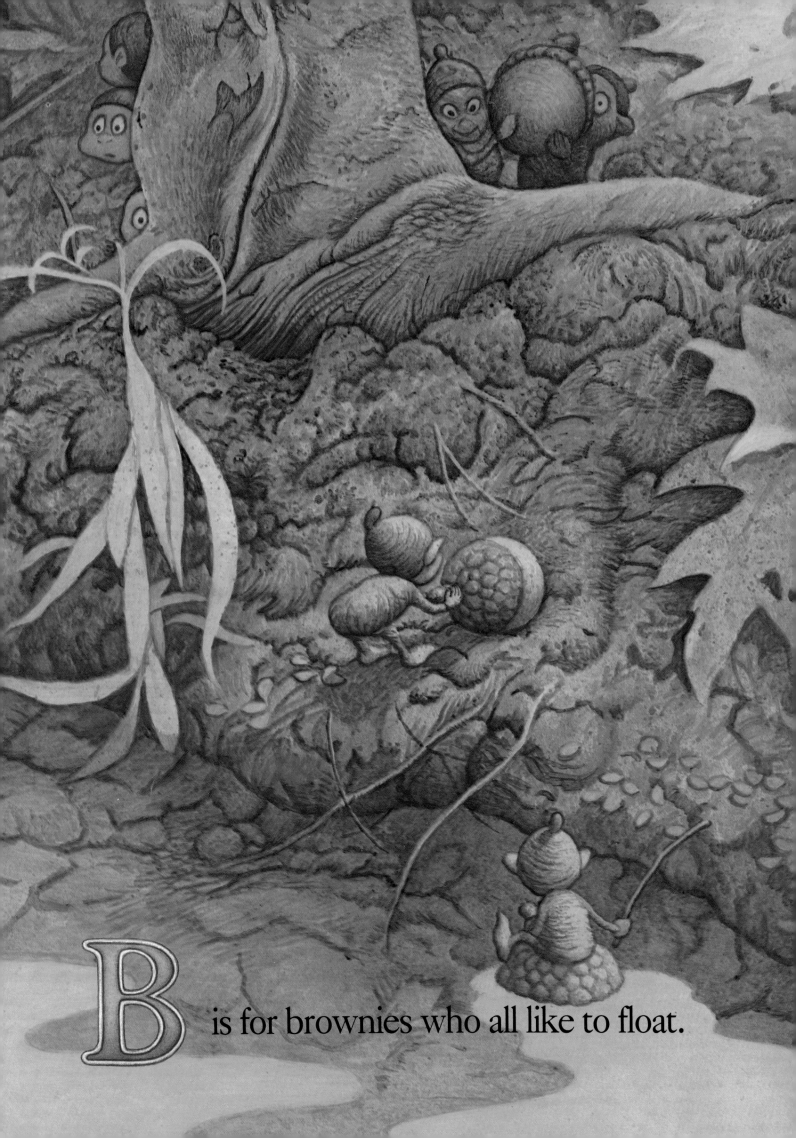

B is for brownies who all like to float.

C is for cabin on a cold forest floor.

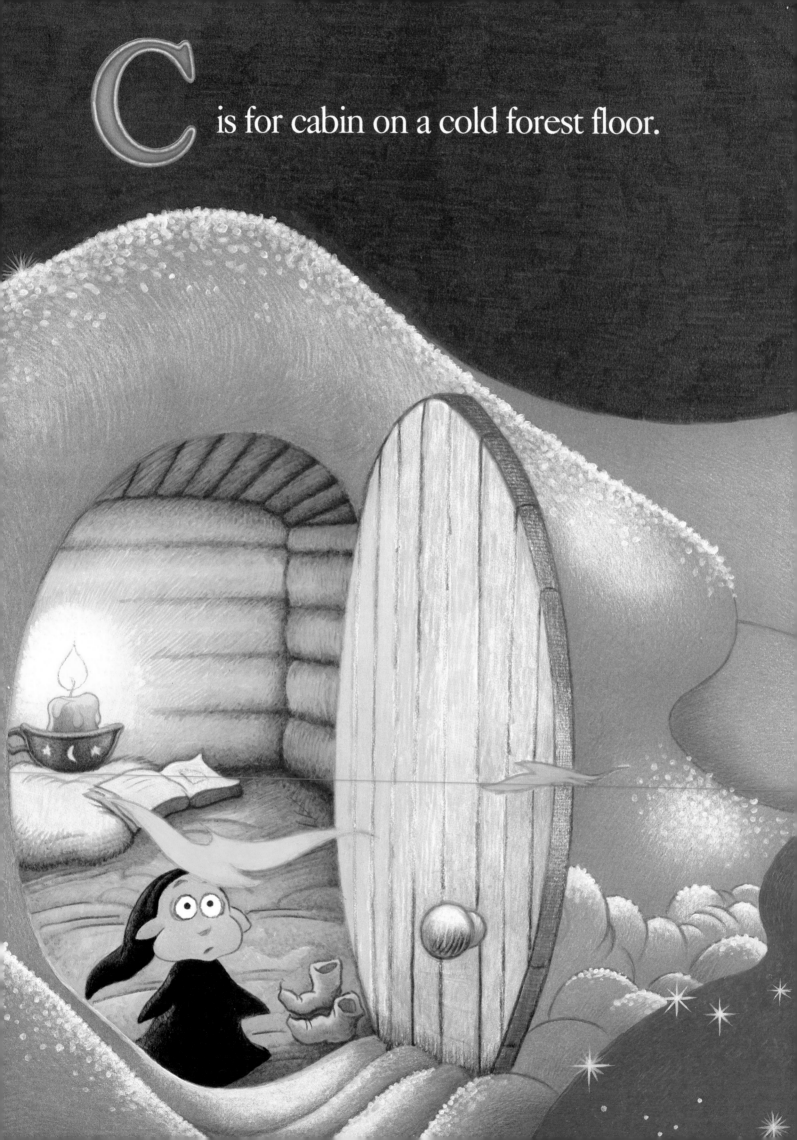

D is for dragon outside the door.

E is for elves who dance round a tree.

F is for fairy tipping over tea.

G is for goblin with a soft yellow nose.

H is for hat as red as a rose.

I is for imps ready for bed.

J is for jumping and bumping their heads.

K is for kite somewhere in the sky.

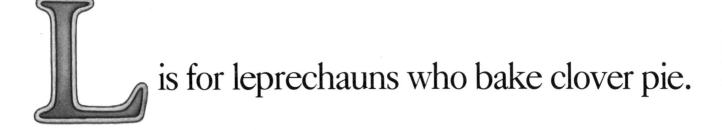

L is for leprechauns who bake clover pie.

M is for mushrooms that grow in the night.

N is for nightgowns on tiny light-sprites.

O is for ogre grumpy and fat.

P is for pixie taking his hat.

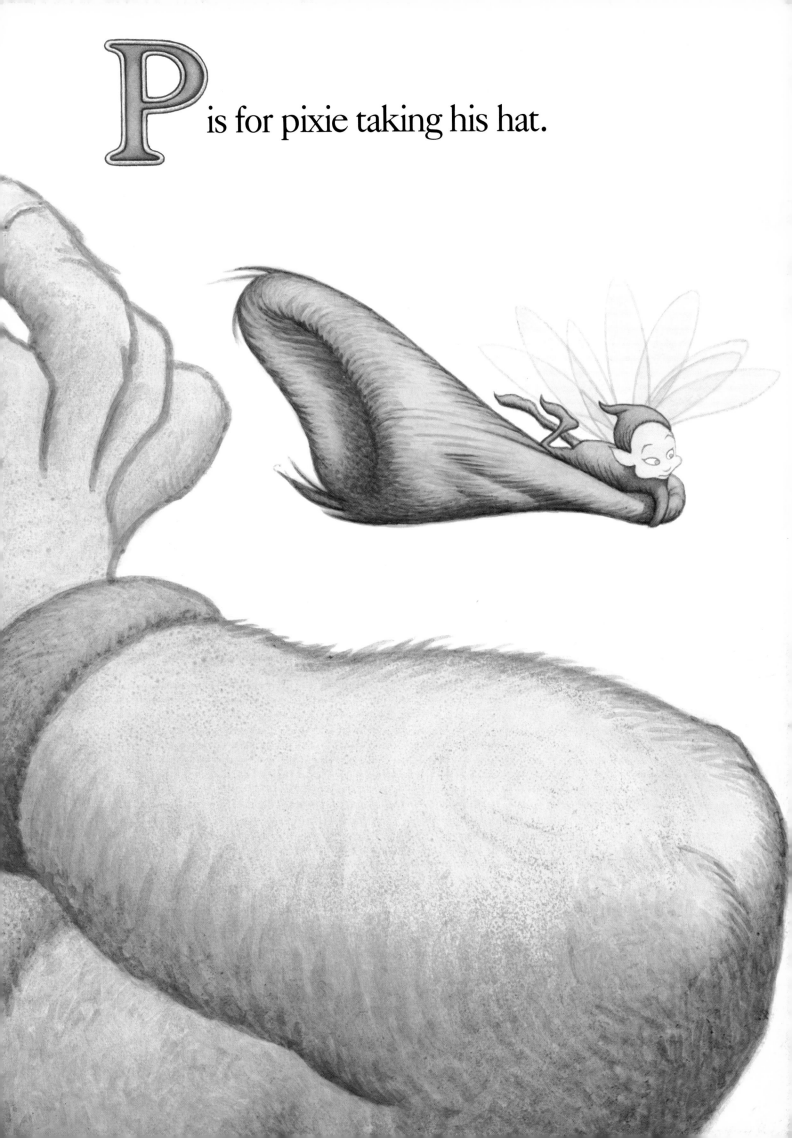

Q is for quilt all fluffy and new.

R is for rainbow sparkling with dew.

 is for strawberries up in the sky.

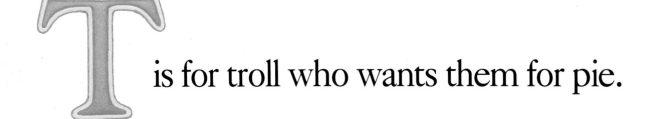

T is for troll who wants them for pie.

U is for umbrellas high in a tree.

V is for violets all cozy round me.

W is for waternymph looking for her mop.

 is for X which marks the spot.

Y is for yarn spun late at night.

Z is for zippers to bundle up tight.

ABCDEFGH
IJKLMNO
PQRSTUV
WXYZ

Design
STEVE PILCHER

Typography
JOHN ELPHICK

Typesetting
COOPER & BEATTY, LIMITED

Separations
S E GRAPHICS

Lithography
G. LYONS LITHO LTD.

Published in Canada
by Hayes Publishing Ltd.
3312 Mainway, Burlington,
Ontario L7M 1A7
ISBN 0-88625-042-0